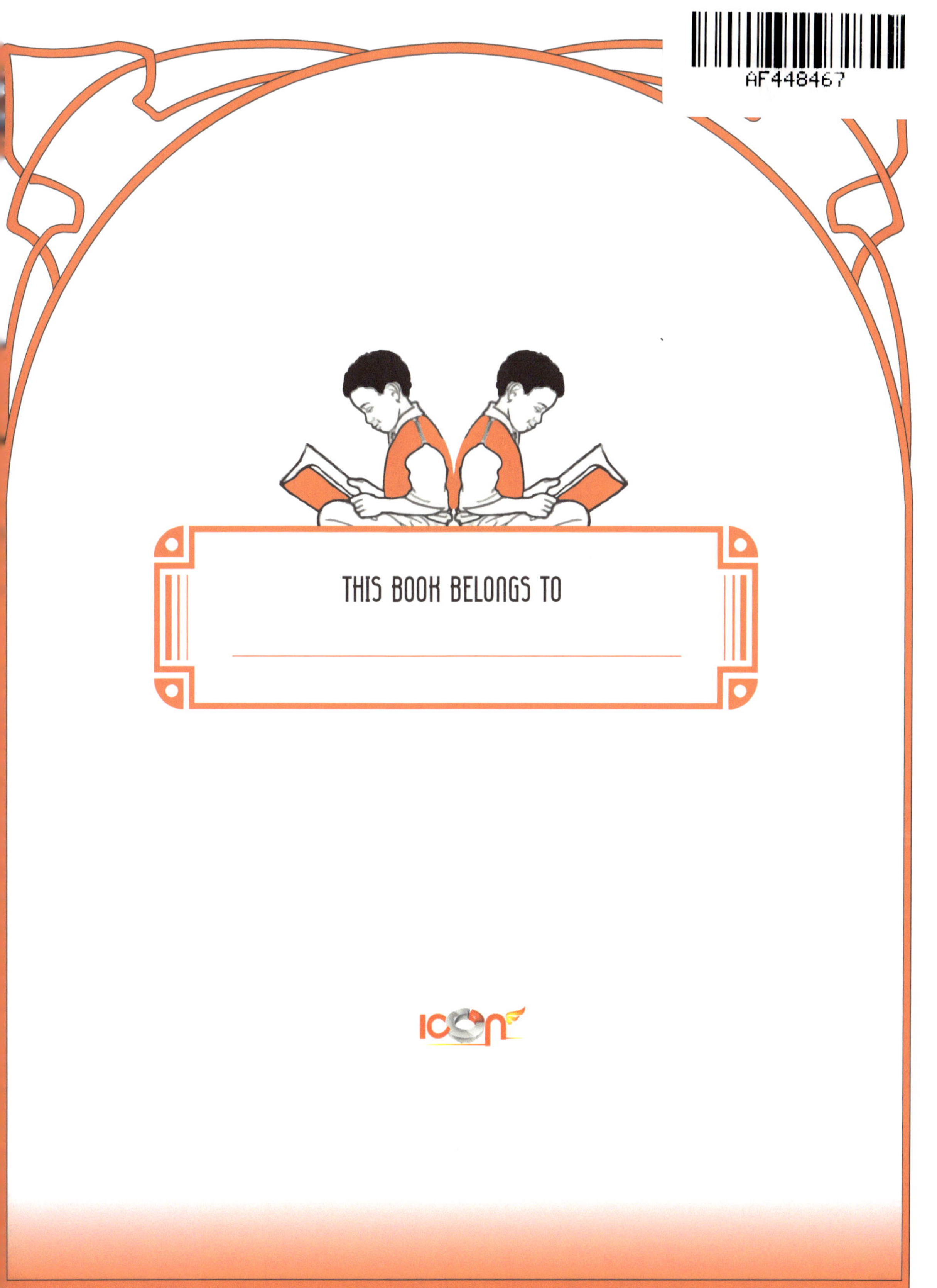
THIS BOOK BELONGS TO

Icon Publishing Limited
P. O. Box OD 972
Odorkor, Accra
Ghana
www.facebook.com/myicongh
www.twitter.com/myicongh
+233 (0)23 3505 055,

iconpublishingltd@gmail.com
iconpublishing@ymail.com
enquiries.icongh@gmail.com



Cover and Interior Design by iCON-gh +233 24 4890 432

ISBN:  978-9988-8566-3-2

# HOW ANANSE SURVIVED THE GREAT FAMINE

## A GHANAIAN FOLKTALE

Dan Odei

Kwame Insaidoo

*This Ghanaian folktale shows how Ananse uses his usual trickery to survive a horrible famine that engulfs his village.*

There was a horrible famine in all over the world, and there was virtually no food anywhere. People everywhere were starving. Ironically, in the middle of the forest, there was a big tree that bore sweet, juicy red fruits, and every day the parrots flew to the top of the tree, ate to their satisfaction, and escaped the brunt of the great famine.

One day Ananse saw the big tree with abundant, red, juicy, ripened fruits and a lot of parrots eating the fruits and singing melodious songs to themselves. Ananse looked at the parrots with envy and decided that something should be done to deprive the parrots of their fruits and enjoyment. Even though he was hungry, he managed to shout loudly enough to be heard by the parrots. "Come down and listen to an important message from almighty God, or else you will all perish!"

The parrots rushed down to Ananse to hear what message God had transmitted through Ananse for them. Ananse swore that God had spoken to him to deliver an important message to the parrots. When the parrots reached where Ananse was, he told them that he would not deliver God's holy message to them until they took him up to eat some of the juicy fruit at the top of the tree. He warned of the dire consequences that would befall them if they refused to listen to the message. The parrots hesitated to take Ananse with them because they knew he was a trickster; but, because they desperately wanted to hear the holy message from God, they agreed to take him to the top of the tree for him to get something to eat.

Many of the parrots removed one of their feathers and gave it to Ananse to enable him to fly to the top of the fruit tree. Behold, the hungry Ananse was able to actually touch the delicious fruits, which made him happy, and without much hesitation he greedily ate to his satisfaction. Then he began to conceive a plan to take over the entire tree for himself. He called all the parrots to the centre of the tree to listen to the message he said was from almighty God. He asked them to make a circle around him so they could all see and hear what he had to say.

Ananse told the parrots, "The tree belongs to my ancestors who lived in the area long, long ago, and they have warned all intruders not to trespass on their personal private property. This is why almighty God has urgently sent me to tell all of you that if you continue to visit this tree, He will bring a plague to kill all of you parrots and wipe you all from the face of the earth." Ananse continued, "So, you see, parrots, if you want to stay alive you better leave the tree and all its fruits alone. Go your miserable way or all of you and your unborn children will be wiped out by almighty God, who is fuming with anger that you parrots would willfully trespass on the personal property of me and my ancestors. Without mincing words, I must order all of you to immediately vacate this tree!"

The parrots were stunned to hear what Ananse had to say, and there was a complete silence in the whole place. Suddenly Ananse seized a big stick and began to whip them; some flew away, but others demanded their feathers back from him before they left. Ananse continued to whack the parrots with his big stick until all of them left the tree with all of its juicy fruits. The area at the top of the tree became silent with only Ananse on top; he had all the fruits at his disposal, but to his amazement, he had no wings left to fly out of the large, tall tree.

*Ananse on top of the tree with the parrots*

Ananse stayed at the top of the tree for days and ate the fruits till there was none left. When he decided to come down, because he had no feathers left to fly with, he had to jump down. He hurt his back, and for three days he could not walk and was forced to stay at the foot of the tree. After a week, he slowly began to walk away from the tree, and eventually he came to a large, roaring, angry river. He could not swim across, given his sickly condition, so he stood there helplessly waiting for someone to assist him.

As he stood at the edge of the river, he saw two crocodiles, husband and wife, splashing water and enjoying their day, swimming and having a great time in the water. When Ananse saw them, he clapped and asked them to come closer to him. When they did, he told them that God had given him a neat and a sacred method for shaving all male crocodiles so they could live longer and enjoy even more fun like the good times they had been having in the water minutes ago. Ananse asked them to carry him across the water so he could give the male crocodile the sacred shave that would insure his longevity. The crocodiles eagerly agreed to carry Ananse across the raging river.

When they crossed the river, Ananse told the crocodile's wife that in order to perform God's sacred shaving ritual on her husband, he needed to be in a room alone with him; when she returned he would reveal the surprise and she would see how her husband had been changed by God's special, sacred shaving technique. The female crocodile agreed and crossed the river back to where the juicy tree was, to see if she could get some of the red, juicy fruits for her husband to enjoy after his sacred shave.

Ananse took the male crocodile to a small room and promised to give him the best sacred shave from God—all his friends would come screaming for the same sacred shave. Ananse assured him that he shouldn't worry about anything. Ananse told the crocodile to lie down with his head facing the ceiling and his eyes closed so that Ananse could invoke the sacred shaving secrets from God, and he further asked the crocodile not to scream if the shaving burned a little. The innocent crocodile did as Ananse told him and closed his eyes. Without wasting time, Ananse took a sharp knife and quickly cut the crocodile's neck; then he wrapped the crocodile's body in a nice cloth, put it on his back, and quickly left the house carrying the body so that when the female crocodile came back she would not see Ananse or her husband again.

Ananse walked for about three miles until he reached the outskirts of a village inhabited by the lion and his friend the lizard. He knew that if he did not think hard, the lion and the lizard would not only take the body of the crocodile away from him, but might also kill him, so Ananse began to sob and cry uncontrollably.

The lion and the lizard came out to meet Ananse and tried to console him, asking him what the matter was and how they could help him. Ananse, still sobbing, told them that his mother was dead and that he was going to bury her alone and needed all the help he could get. "I am very miserable now that my mother has died," he said, "and I want to join her, but as a man I must be strong enough to bury her with dignity."

The lion felt sympathetic toward Ananse and actually gave him several pieces of gold to help him pay for the burial of his mother. Ananse thanked them and bade them farewell; then he moved hurriedly away from their village, saying under his breath, "You damned fools, thanks for your gold. You think you are strong, but I have successfully outmaneuvered all of you strong and fierce animals."

The lizard told the lion he should be careful of Ananse, asking, "Did you actually see the body of Ananse's mother?" The lizard warned the lion that Ananse was extremely cunning; he suggested that they should go and demand to see the body of Ananse's mother with their own eyes.

The lion agreed with the lizard's idea of demanding to see what was supposedly the body of Ananse's mother. They ran after Ananse and demanded to see the body. But as Ananse got ready to speak, the lion ripped open the cloth covering the body and, alas, saw the neatly wrapped body of the crocodile, which he seized from Ananse. The lion and the lizard dragged Ananse back to the house and tied his legs to a pole in the house, while the lizard laughed at his supposed intelligence and wisdom and called him a deceitful bastard.

The lizard prepared a delicious soup with all the crocodile's meat, and when the lion and the lizard got ready to eat, Ananse, who was still tied up, looked at the soup and began to laugh uncontrollably. He continued to laugh and laugh until the lion asked him to explain to them what was so funny about their food. Ananse replied that the soup would taste better if he gave both of them the sacred shave from God that would enhance their taste buds. The lion thought the idea was great because all the food he had eaten for the past week hadn't tasted so good, so he released Ananse from the pole and asked for the sacred shave.

Ananse took the lion to the back of the house to give him the sacred shave and asked the lizard to watch the soup to prevent flies from dropping into it and infecting it with dangerous diseases. Ananse told the lion that because of the delicate nature of the sacred shave he should lean against the tree and tie his legs and arms to the pole with a small rope to prevent him from moving around, which would mess up the quality of the sacred shave.

Ananse tied the lion tightly to the huge tree in their backyard and made sure the lion could not escape. Then he told the lion to rest while he went to get the special sacred shaving blade to complete a beautiful shave for him. When Ananse went back to the house, he saw the lizard waiting for his turn to receive God's sacred shaving. Ananse assured him that the Lion was almost finished, so he should prepare for his own shave and stand by the pole inside the house. The lizard did as he was told, and Ananse tied him to the pole; he made sure, however, that the Lizard could not escape.

Ananse then went to the bushes and got a large whip, and then went to the back of the house where the lion was tied up, and gave him a good beating to his bare back, until blood oozed from his buttocks and back. Ananse said to the lion, "You fool; you thought I would let you take my hard-earned crocodile meat from me."

He turned to the lizard as well and whipped him many times until he begged for mercy. Ananse continued to beat him until he was about to collapse. Ananse said to them both, "You damned animals are fools and would not learn your lesson. Next time, don't try to double cross me to take my delicious crocodile meat from me."

Ananse settled down and ate all the meat and drank some soup, and  then threw the rest of the hot soup on both the lion and the lizard before finally leaving the village.

*Ananse giving the tied lion and lizard a good beating*

After about three or four days, the lion and the lizard finally succeeded in freeing themselves from the ropes because the rain had made the ropes slippery. But they both swore that they would tear Ananse into pieces when they got their hands on him.

One day the lion saw Ananse tilling the soil to plant his corn farm. Hurriedly Ananse asked the lion whether he was looking for the deceitful Ananse who was going about tricking innocent people, including himself. Ananse said, "That deceitful Ananse has stolen most of my corn from my farm, and I am looking to kill him myself. So, if you find him, let me know and I will help you to kill him." The lion, not knowing that he was speaking to the same Ananse who had tricked him, left him to look for "the deceitful Ananse."

But as he was turning the corner, the lizard began to scream and point to Ananse, telling the lion, "That is the Ananse we are looking for! That is the deceitful Ananse, because there is only one Ananse in the whole wide world! Please, Lion, catch him—don't let him escape this time!" The lion jumped to snatch Ananse up in his jaws, but Ananse jumped up higher into the big tree and began weaving his web—and

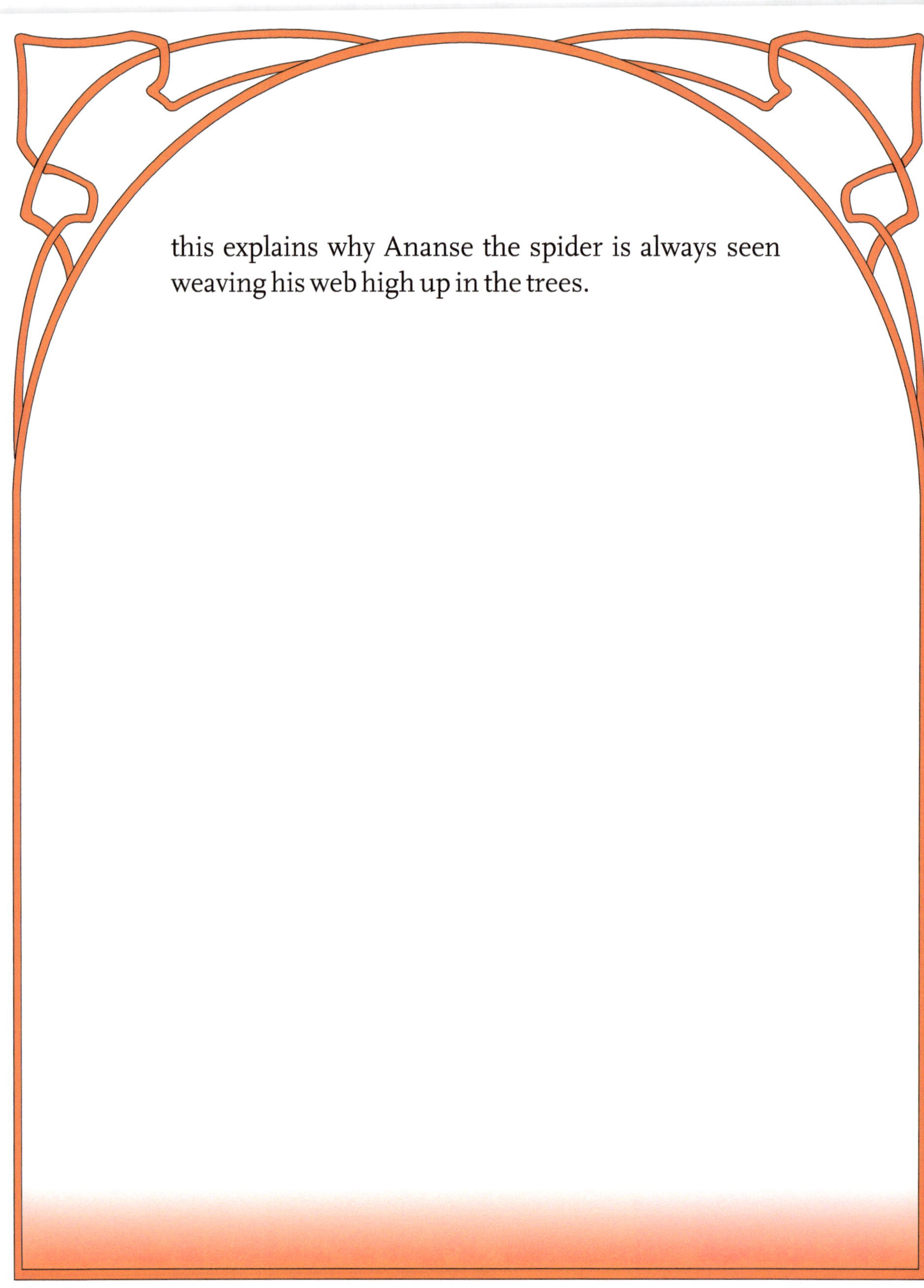

this explains why Ananse the spider is always seen weaving his web high up in the trees.

The moral here is to observe the deception that wicked people play on innocent and naive people to get their way, just like Ananse did to all the other characters in the story. We should also be careful of those who use God's name to deceive others in order to amass their wealth and exploit gullible women for sex and money. You see, the parrots genuinely but naively believed Ananse's so-called message from God and gave their feathers to him only to be driven from their fruit tree in the midst of the terrible famine. The poor innocent crocodile having fun with his wife in their river suffered death at the hands of Ananse because of his gullibility.

Answer the following questions:

1. a) Why did the parrots obey Ananse's instructions?

   b) How did Ananse bring down the parrots from the tree?

2. a) What trick did Ananse play on the parrots?

   b) How did he drive them away?

3. What happened to Ananse when he jumped down from the tall tree?

4. a) How did Ananse trick the two crocodiles?

   b) What happened to the male crocodile?

   c) How was Ananse able to cross the raging river?

5. a) What trick did Ananse play on the lion and his lizard friend?

   b) What made the lion feel sympathetic towards Ananse?

6. Who prepared food with the crocodiles body?

7. a) What did Ananse do to the tied lion and lizard?

   b) Who freed the lion and his lizard friend?

   c) When they returned one day to kill Ananse, what trick did he (Ananse) play on them?

8. What made Ananse jump up to the big tree?

9. What have you learned from this folktale?

10. Find the meaning of the following words in the dictionary and use them in sentences of your own.

i. Engulf

ii. Virtually

iii. Ironically

iv. Deprive

v. Perish

vi. Dire

vii. Trespass

viii. Plague

ix. Fuming

x. Mincing

xi. Stunned

xii. Whack

xiii. Longevity

xiv. Console

xv. Sobbing

xvi. Outmaneuvered

xvii. Enhance

xviii. Oozed

11. How many adjectives are in the first paragraph of the passage? List all of them.

12. Give synonyms for each of the underlined words below:

    a. in the <u>middle</u> of the forest

    b. He warned of the dire <u>consequences</u>

    c. I must <u>order</u> all of you to immediately vacate this tree

    d. He was waiting for someone to <u>assist</u> him

    e. all his friends will come <u>screaming</u>

    f. then he moved <u>hurriedly</u> away

    g. Ananse tied the lion to the <u>huge</u> tree

Answer the questions here.

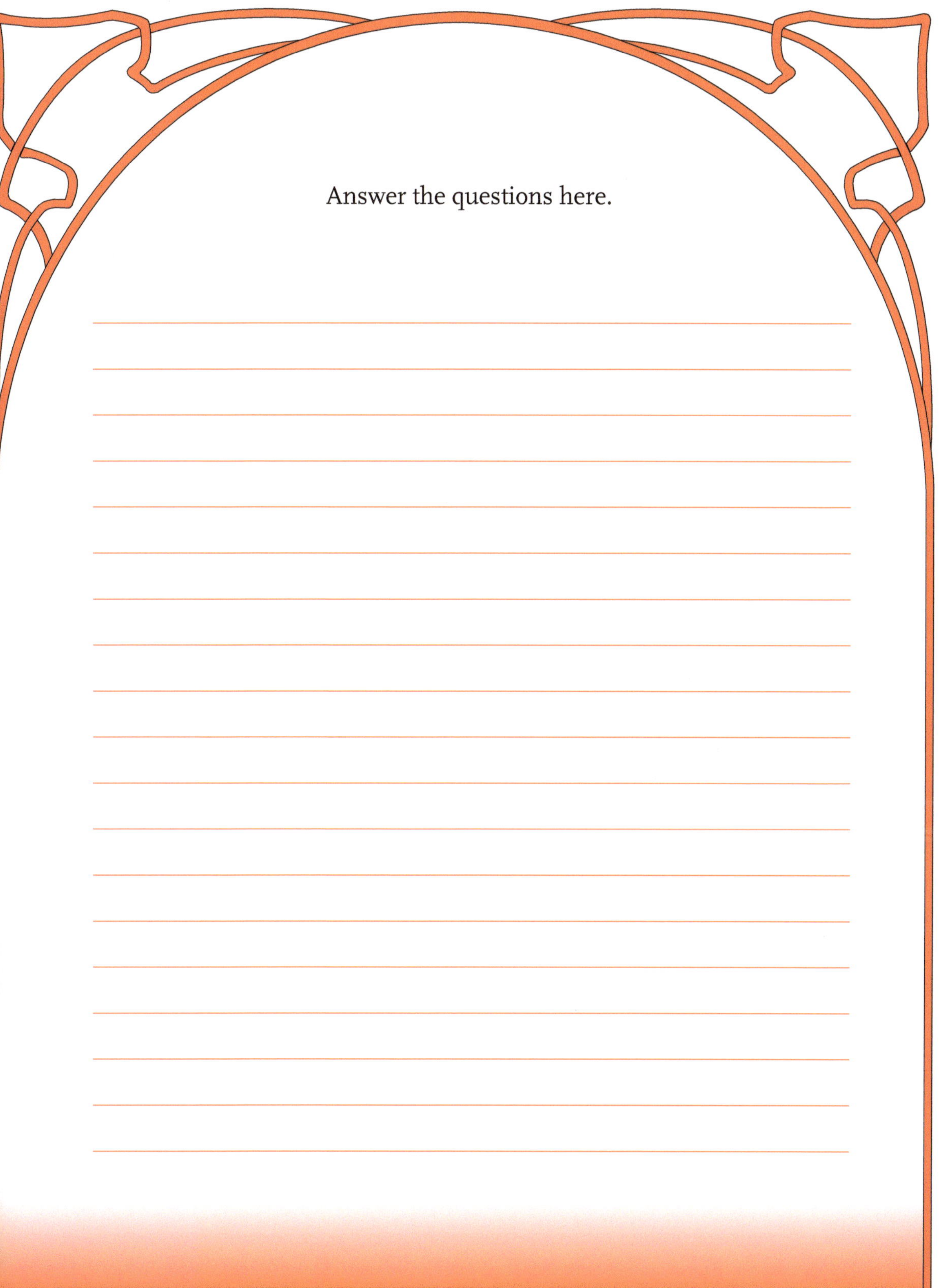

Answer the questions here.

Answer the questions here.

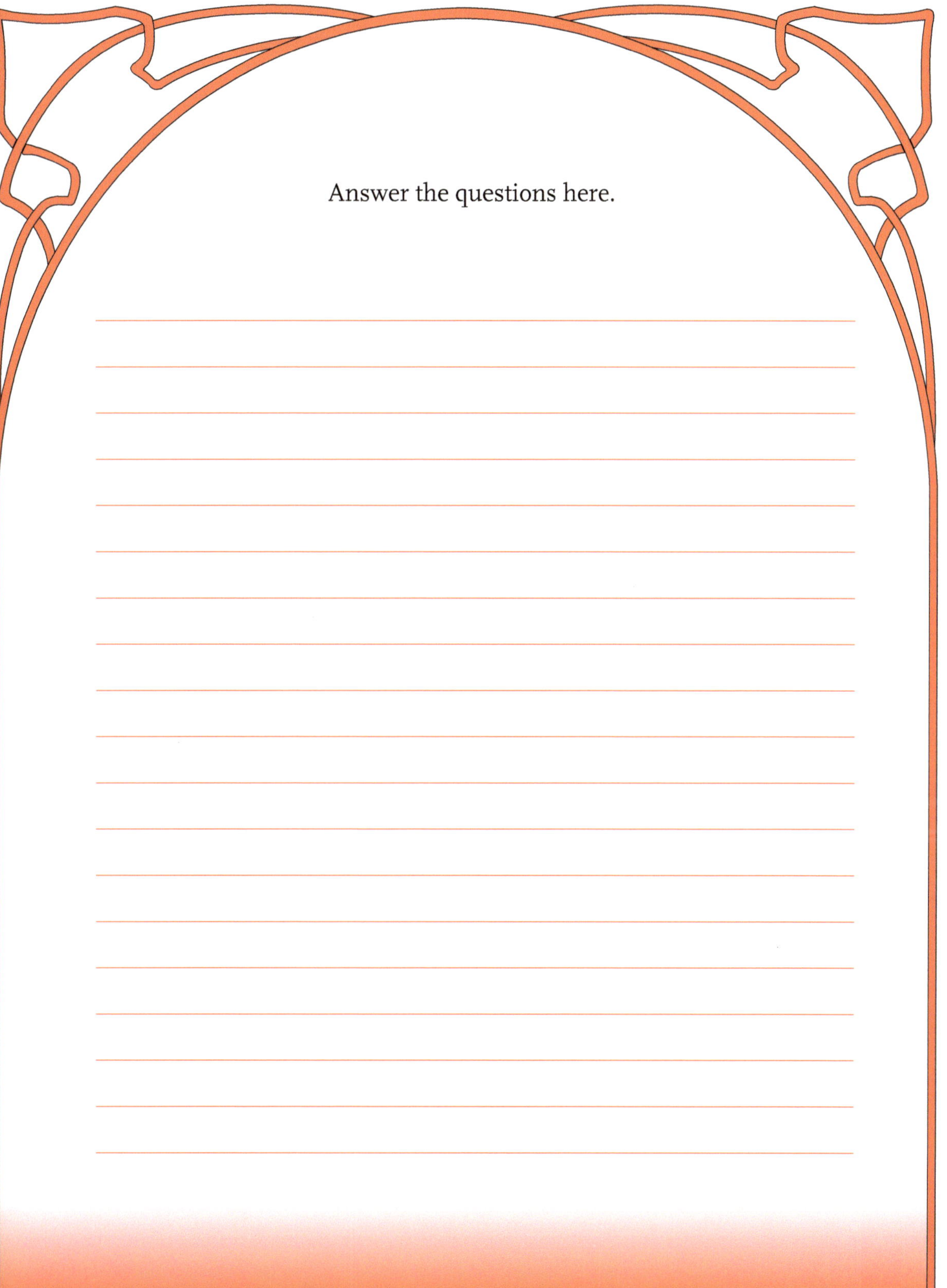

Answer the questions here.